For Paul

First U.S. Edition
3 4 5 6 7 8 9 10
Library of Congress Catalog Card Number 80-84971
ISBN 0-688-00552-7
ISBN 0-688-00553-5 (lib. bdg.)

Jan Ormerod

Sunshine

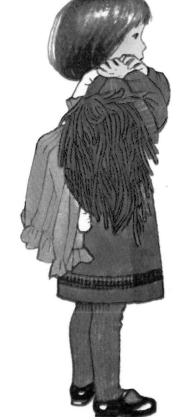

Lothrop, Lee & Shepard Books • New York

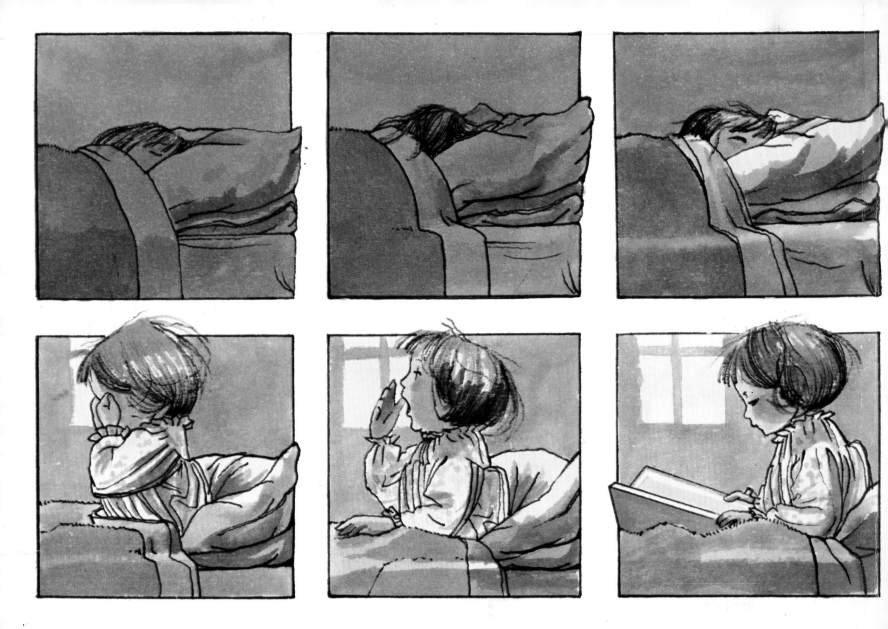

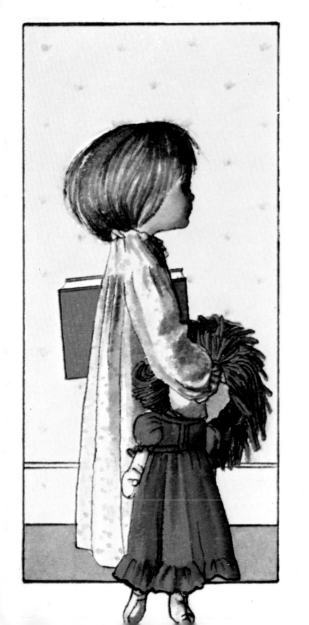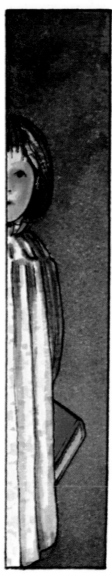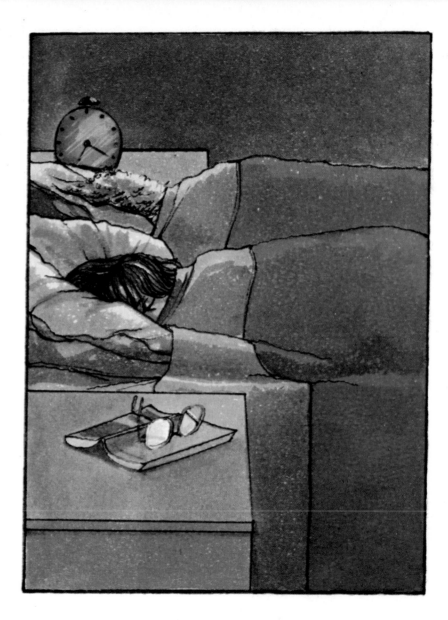

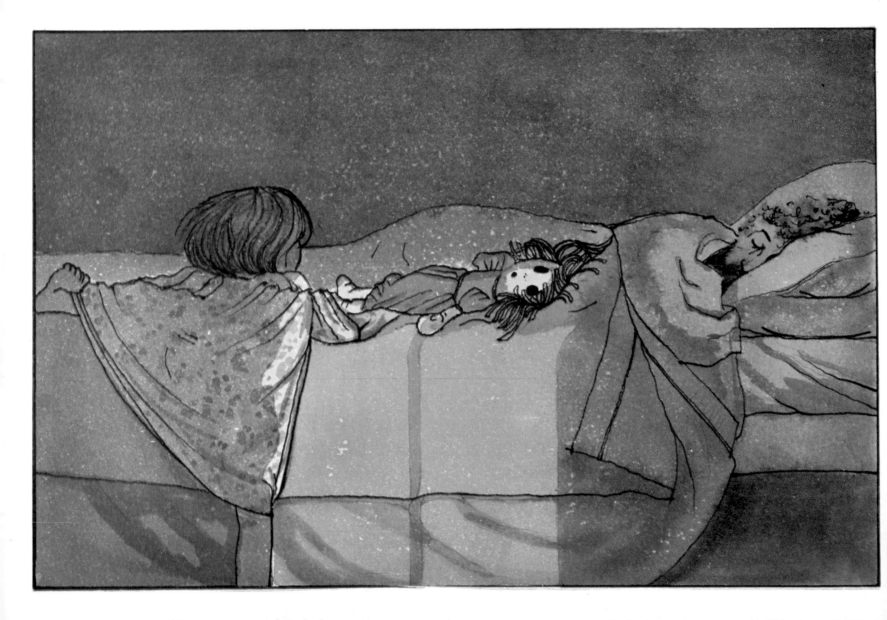

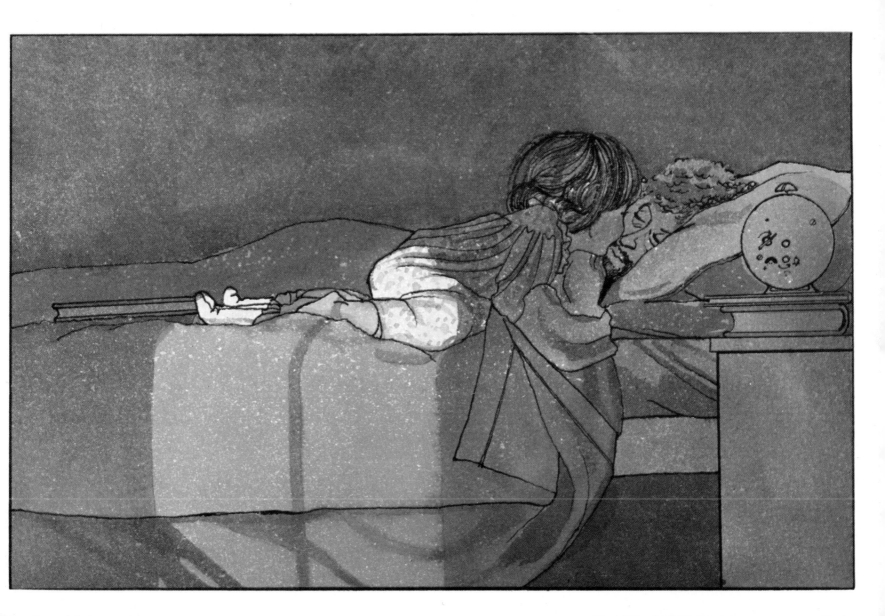

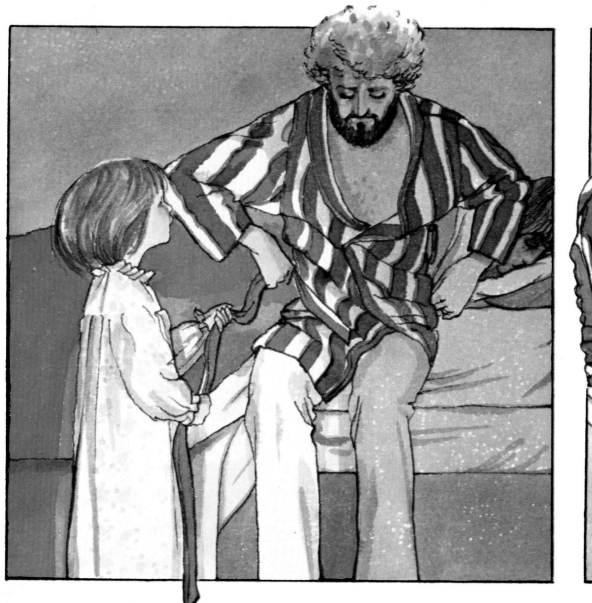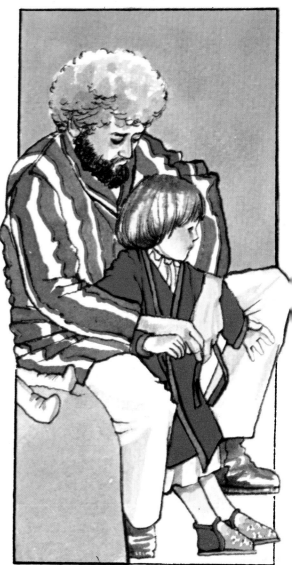

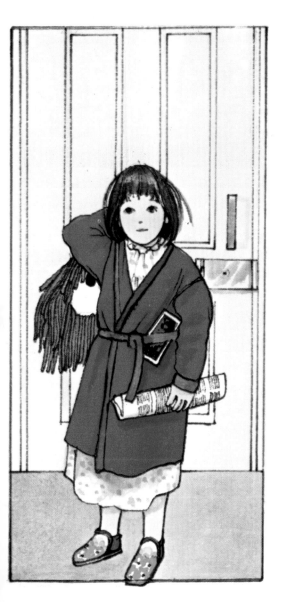
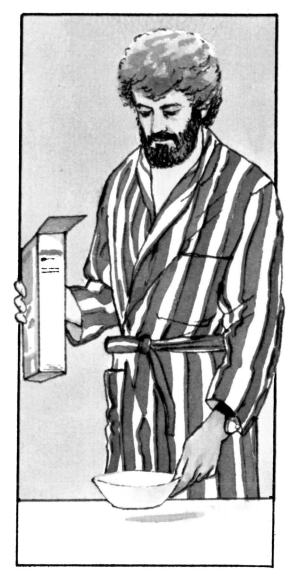
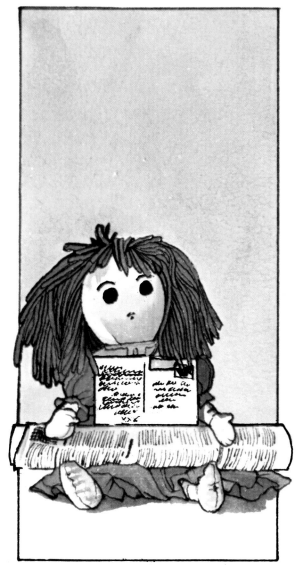

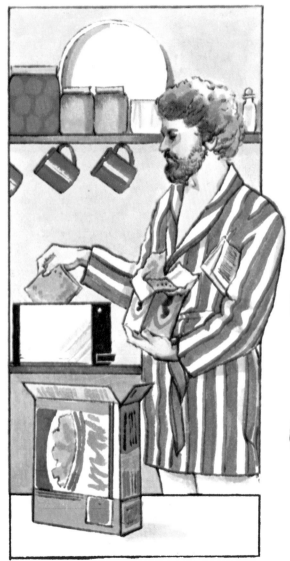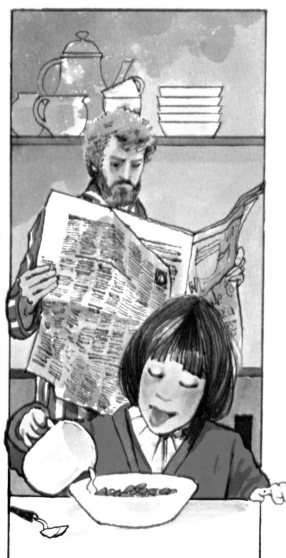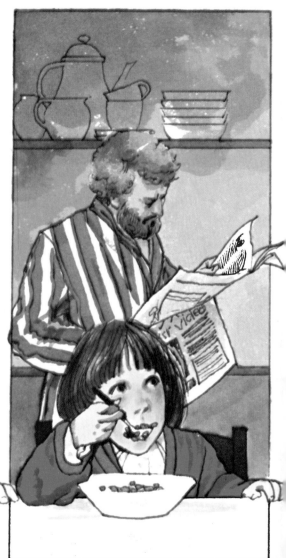

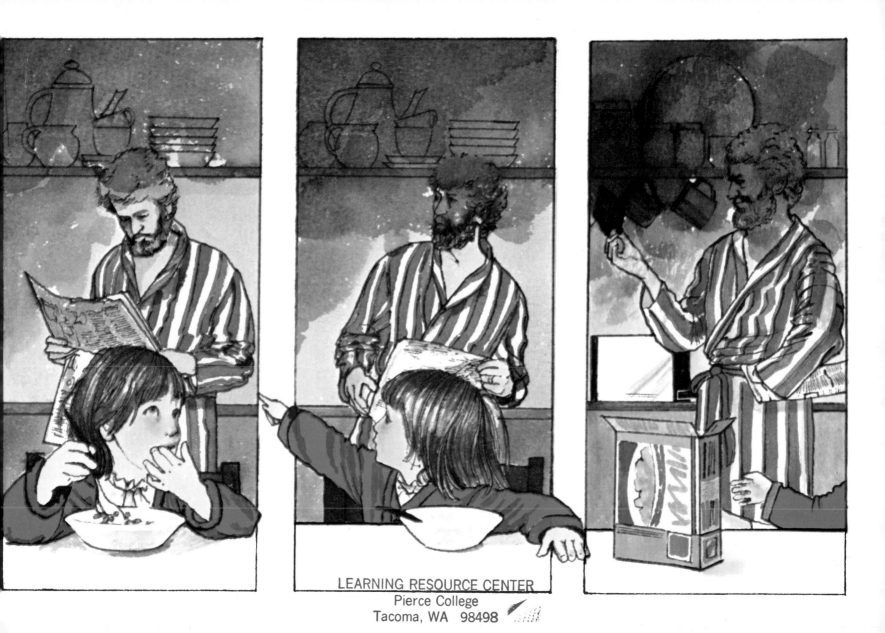

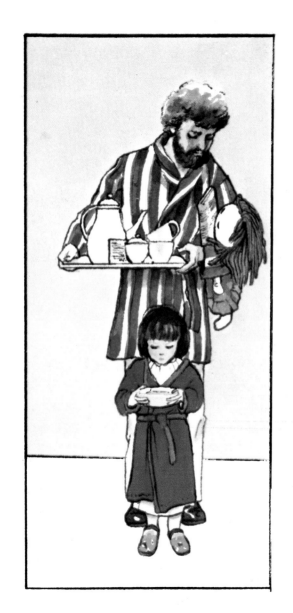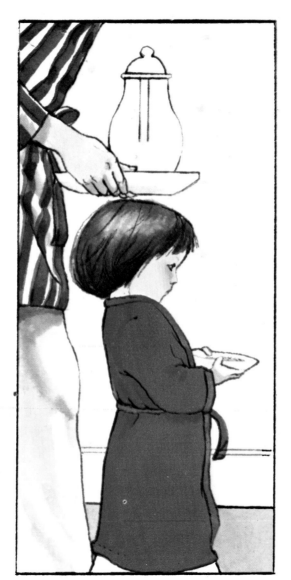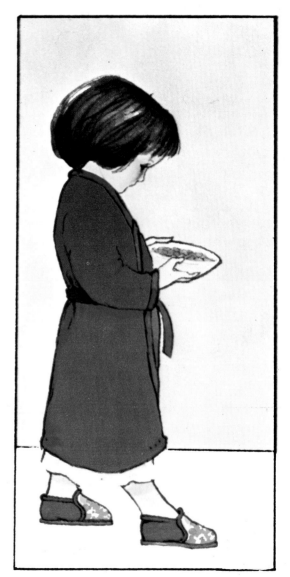

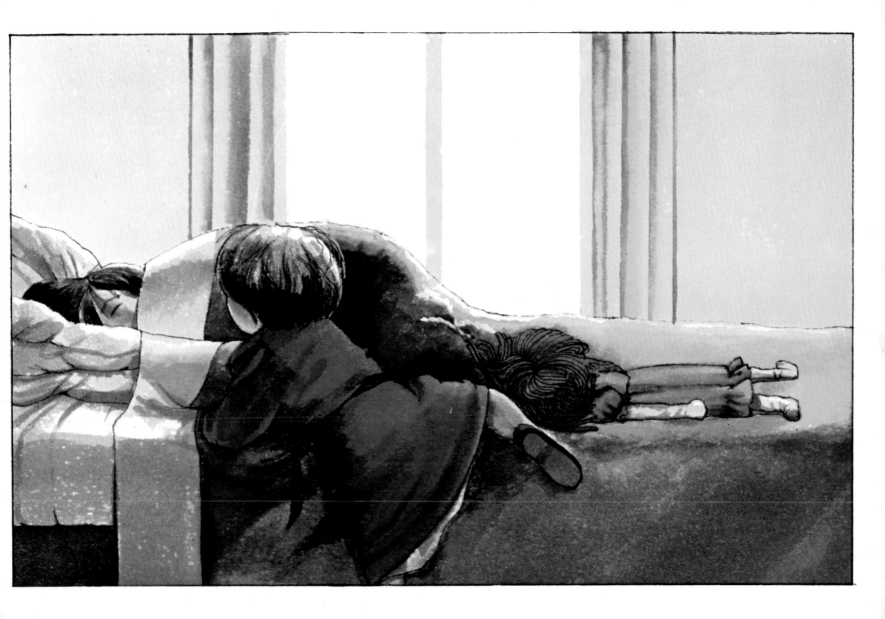

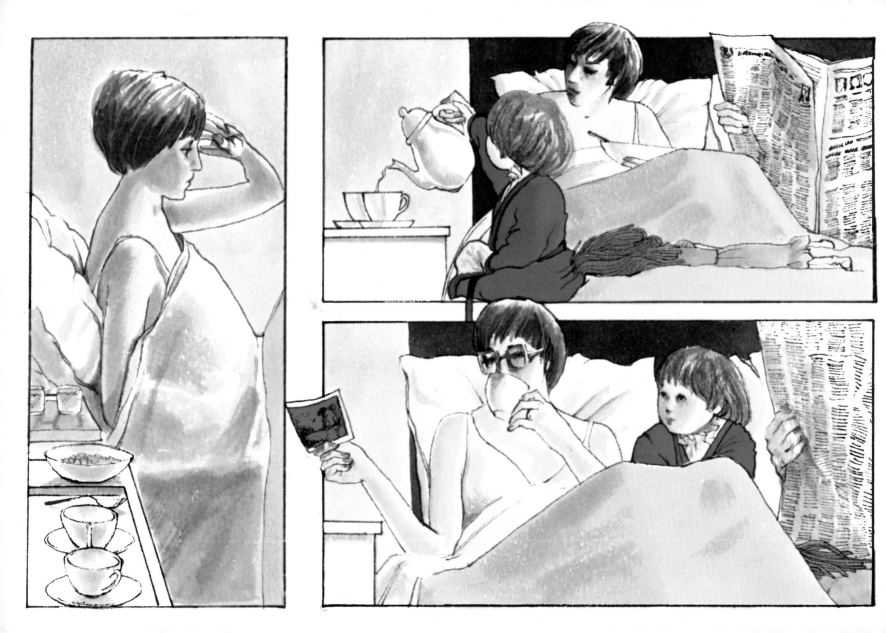

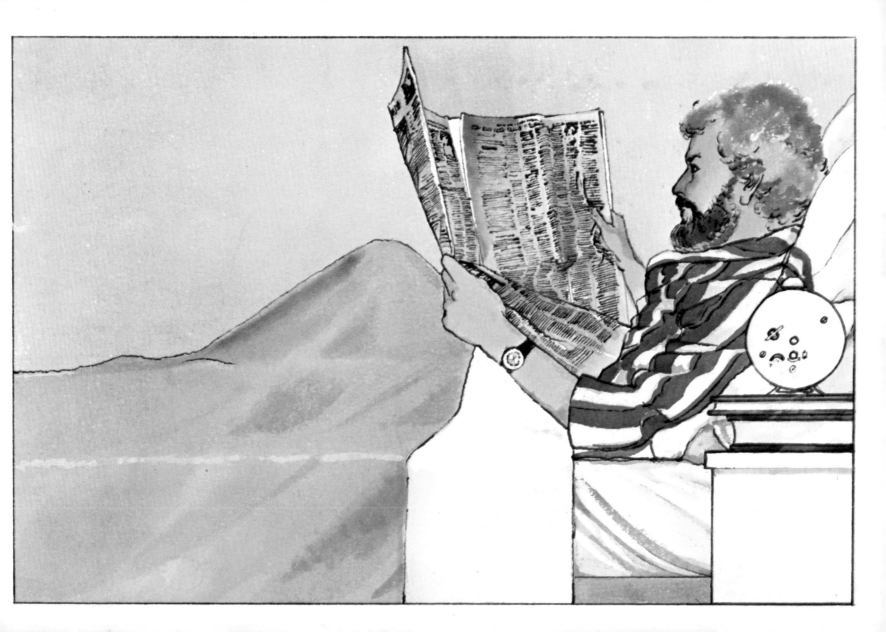

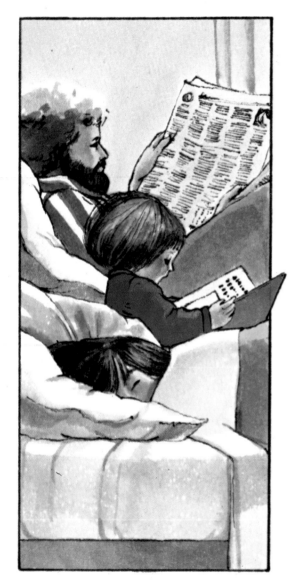
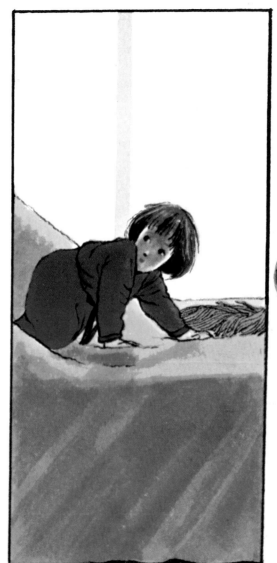
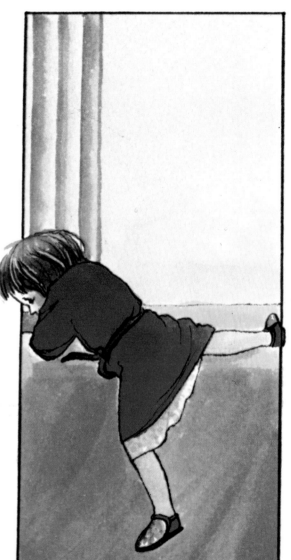

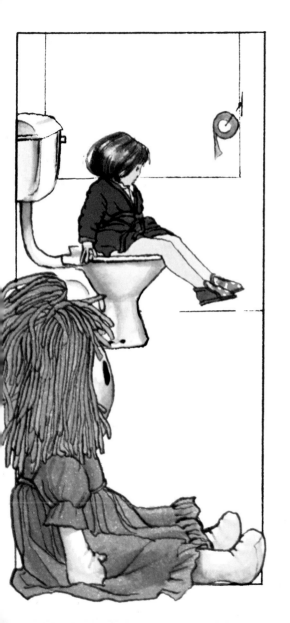
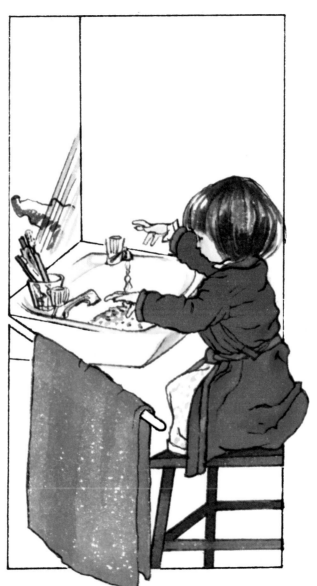
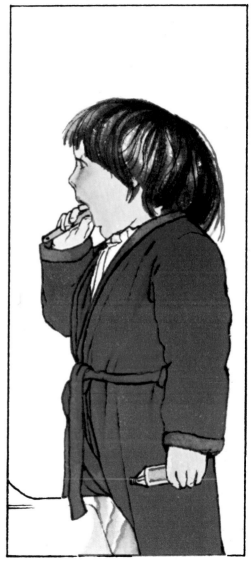

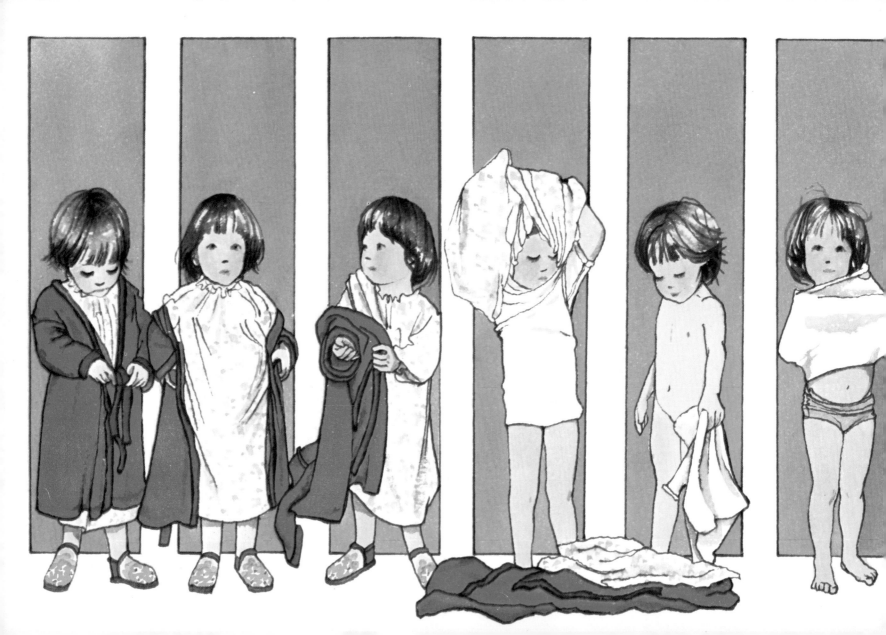

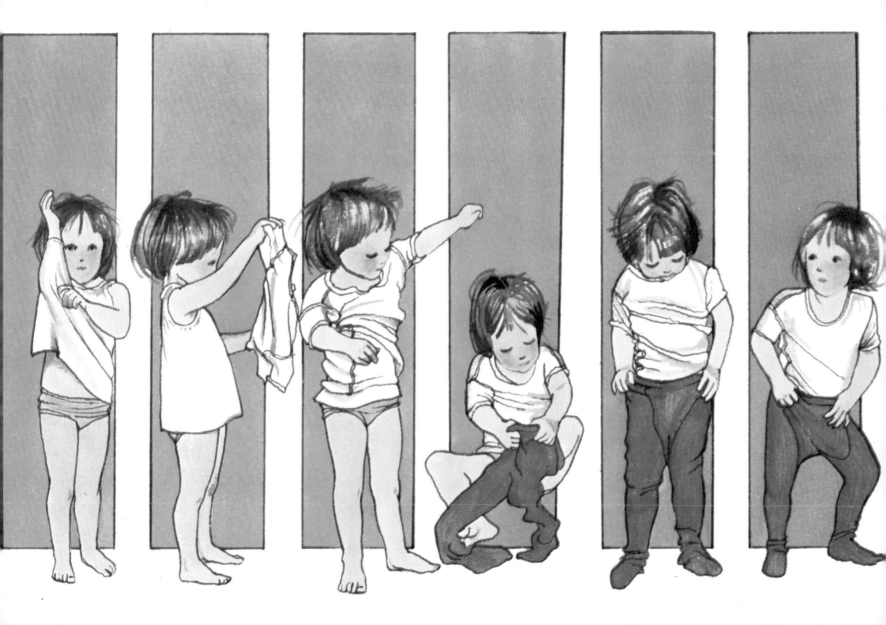

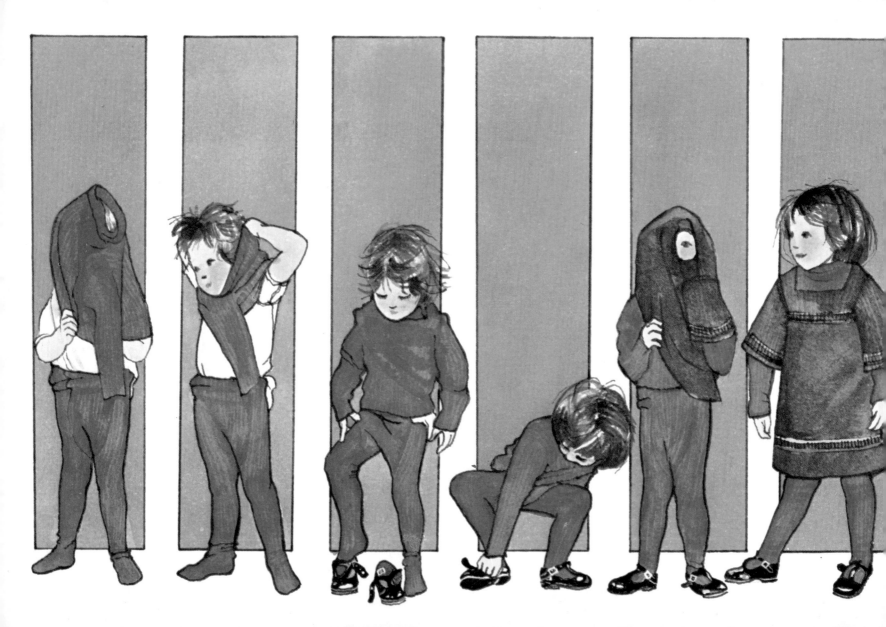

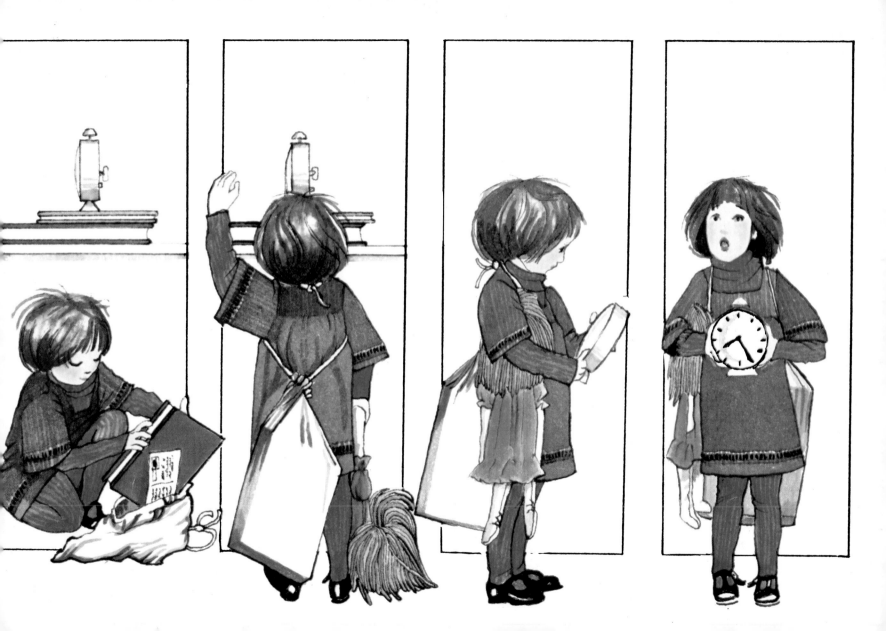

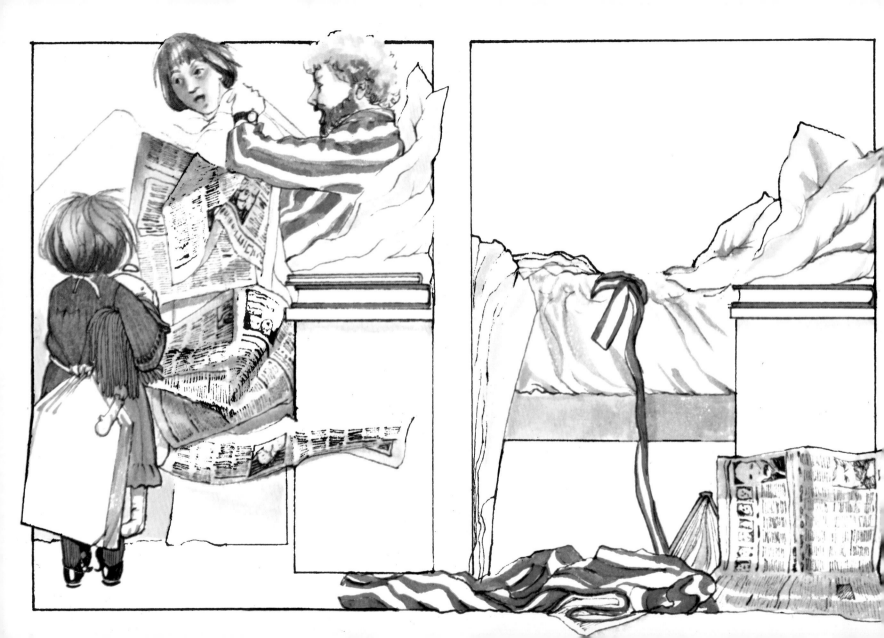

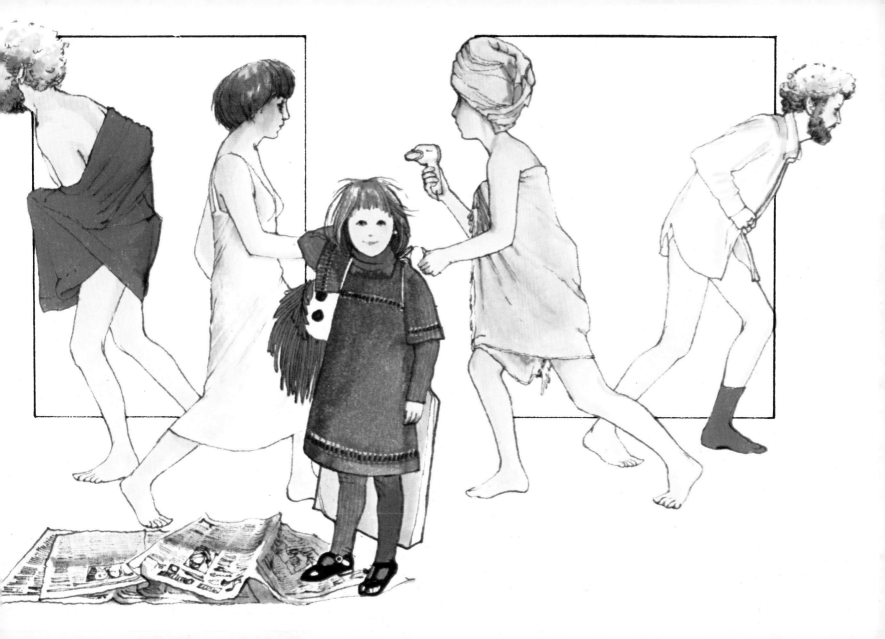

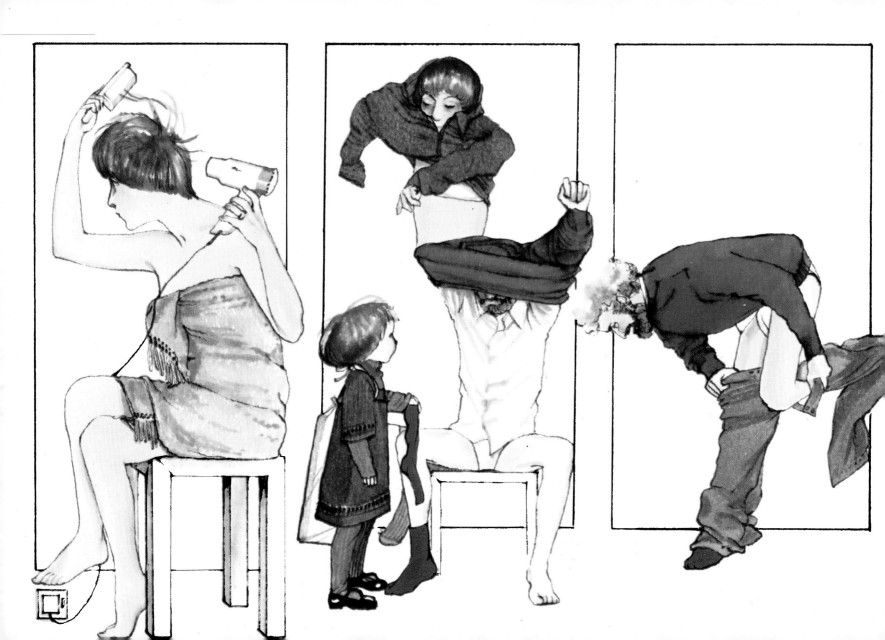

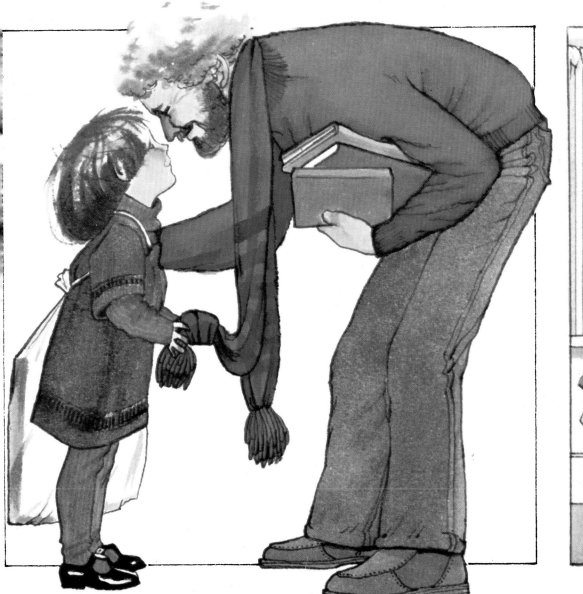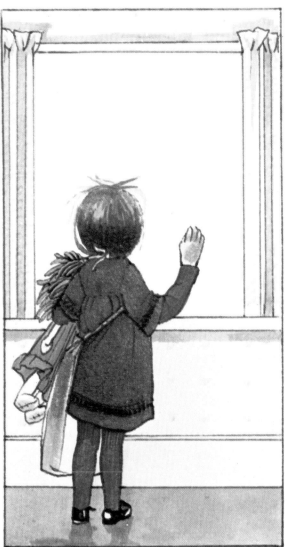

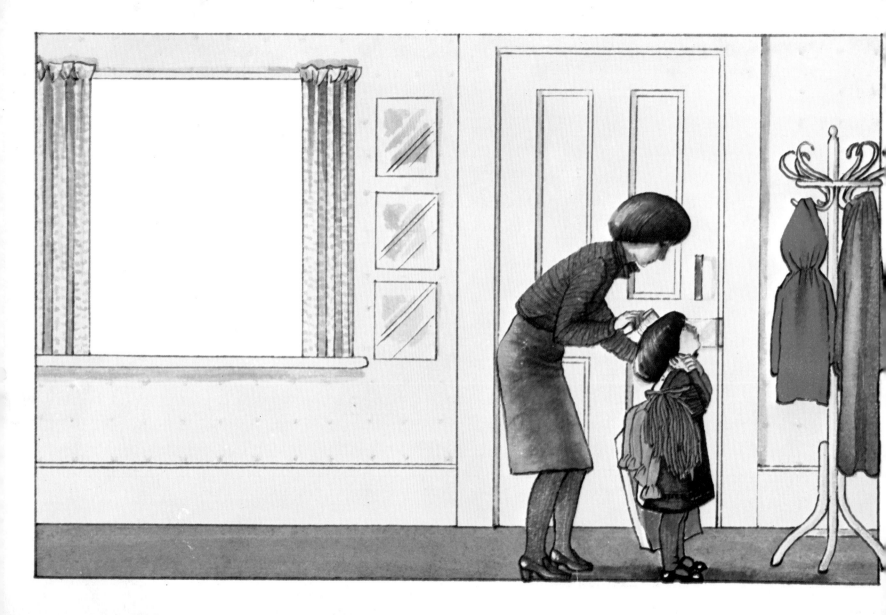

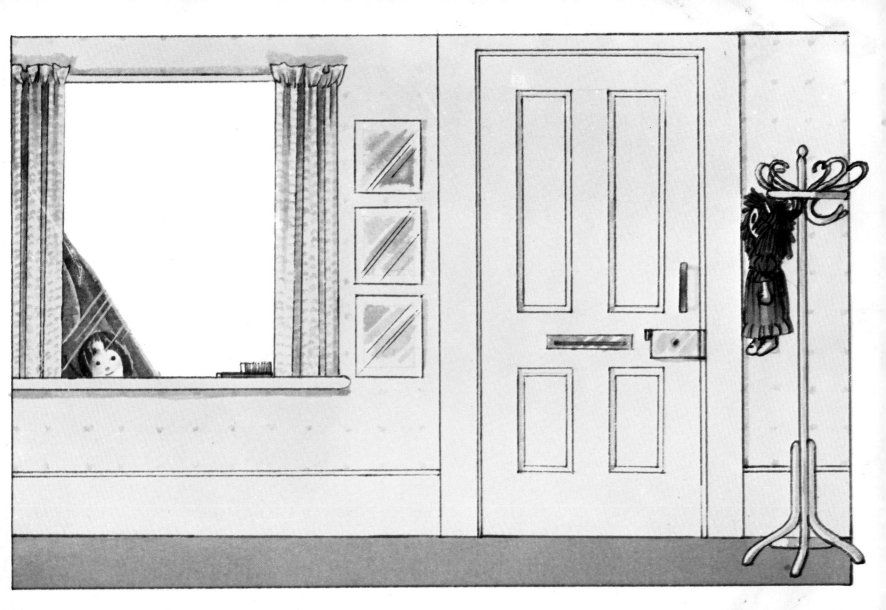

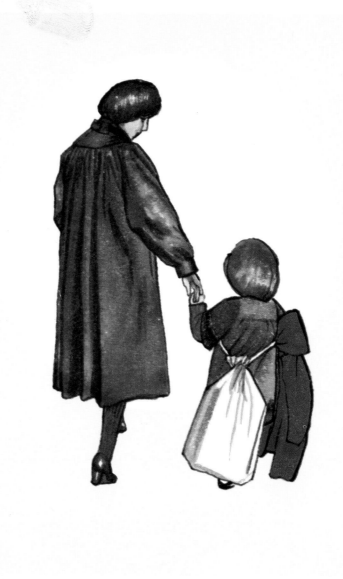